This Book Belongs to:

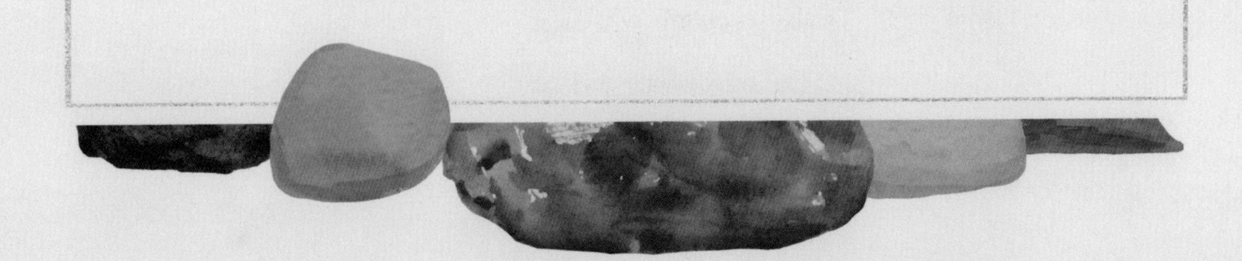

The Great Easter Egg Robbery

ISBN: 979-8-43606-294-5

First printing edition 2022.

www.stephanieoconnorbooks.com

Easter was just around the corner.
The Easter Bunny had collected lots of hen and duck eggs from the farm and was busy making painted eggs
- dashing and splashing the colors on them -
to deliver as presents to all of his friends.

No one had ever seen such wonderful painted eggs, and it took the Easter Bunny many days to make them. But he always made them for Easter, for they were bright and cheery to look at.

Then, every night when he went to sleep in his house under the ground, he would always leave the eggs outside so that the air and early sun would dry them while he slept.

You wouldn't think that anyone would be so foolish as to steal from the Easter Bunny.

But one night a rascal wolf crept near to look and saw the lovely eggs. His eyes glittered with greed.

"I need these eggs for myself, and I'm going to get them because they will look so colorful in my lair," he said to himself.

He made up his mind that he would steal the painted eggs, so he crept behind a tree to hide. Then he waited in the black darkness until he was sure the rabbit was asleep before creeping closer.

Little by little, the wolf crawled toward the house. Then he waited a long time, listening until he heard the rabbit was snoring.

Finally, he crept to where the eggs lay. Then, very cautiously, he tucked one of the precious eggs under his chin. He knew just how to move the eggs without breaking them.

All night long, the wicked wolf went back and forth, taking the painted eggs.

When finally he had taken the last egg, he ran for the last time over hills and valleys, across the river, toward his lair, laughing at his smartness as he ran.

It had been a long night, and soon he grew tired.

"Ha!" he said to himself, "I have all the eggs now. I will sleep easy now. How fun it was to steal from the Easter Bunny!"

The next morning, the Easter Bunny went out and found all of the eggs missing!
"Dear me! Fur and whiskers, where have they gone?" he said to himself.

He thought directly of Mr Owl, the wisest creature in the woods, and went to find him.

Mr Owl was at home, sitting on a branch of a tall tree. When the Easter Bunny told his story, he blinked his round eyes and turned his head all the way around to look at him.

"If anyone has stolen your painted Easter eggs, it must be the wolf, for he was terribly busy last night running backwards and forwards all night. His laughter could be heard for quite some distance." said Mr Owl.

The Easter Bunny returned home and examined the ground, and of course, he saw the wolf's footprints.

He hung his head, for he had never been so sad. It would soon be Easter, and he was thinking that he had never had an Easter without painted eggs in his life.

"Ah! All my work has been for nothing.

Easter is ruined!"

he cried.

Just then, hippety-hop came the sound of two of his friends. He didn't want any visitors. So he turned to look back at his little stubby tail and said,

"Please go away, I'm the Easter Bunny, but I've nothing left for Easter."

Seeing no eggs, his friends cried.

"Oh no! No eggs for Easter? That will never do! Where are they?"

The Easter Bunny twitched his long ears to and fro and said, "The wolf has taken the eggs away."

Then with tears in his eyes, he told him that Easter was ruined.

"Then you must go there and take the eggs back," said his friends.

The Easter Bunny replied, "What can I do? I am only one rabbit against a wolf. He would catch me."

This answer gave his friends a plan!

"We'll have to help the Easter Bunny. For soon, it will be Easter!" his friends said.

When they told the other animals what had happened, they all wanted to help, but trembled because they were afraid.

"We'd like to help beyond a doubt. But would it be wise?
The wolf is very dangerous to us.
He's very scary and bigger than us."

But the rabbits told them,
"The wolf is a clever thief but a mighty fool as well, to steal from the kind Easter Bunny and expect to hide away. Doesn't he know that Easter belongs to all of us? If he steals from the kind Easter Bunny, he steals from us all.

And together, we are bigger than him!"

Then the most astonishing thing happened!

"Yes! Yes!"

shouted the animals eagerly.

Then, listening intently, the animals plotted to take the eggs back like a band of robbers.

And what a plan they had!

You may be sure that no one stayed up late that night. Instead, they all went to bed early to save their strength for the great egg robbery.

When the next day came, the animals all got up at sunrise.

Everyone was going to help the Easter Bunny. Some of the animals traveled alone, and others took the whole family.

There were rabbits, squirrels and mice.
There were deer and pigs, the Easter Bunny's best friends, and many others.

And as they went on their journey, they said to every animal as they passed along.

As soon they were close to the wolf's lair, they hid in some bushes and listened a long time before they dared to go closer.

Mr Owl thought it would be easiest to distract the wolf, so they collected a pile of bones and set a fire. Up curled the smoke from the fire through the forest and soon the wolf, who happened to be roaming through the woods, saw and smelt something.

He wagged his tail and looked, then howled, with his eyes fixed upon the rising smoke.

"Ah, how fortunate!" he said, "Dinner!" and he licked his lips.

It didn't take him a second to find the food, pull the bones from the fire to cool, and then such a feast he had.

The wolf ate until he became sleepy. Then he lay down on the forest floor and went to sleep.

Then, as soon as the wolf was asleep, all of the forest animals crept to his lair and peeked inside.

All about the wolf's lair were the beautiful eggs painted by the Easter Bunny.

One by one, they went in, and as quick as they could, the robbers set about the work of dividing up the eggs to carry. Then, whisk! jump! as quick as a wink they each took an egg, and were off, carrying it over their shoulders.

Then away they went—running as fast as they could—straight ahead, looking at nothing, hearing nothing, stopping at nothing.

But just as they were leaving, who should come bounding after them but the wolf.

Returning to his lair he saw the commotion and chased after the animals. But quick as a flash, they raced away.

Everybody ran, and the wolf, not knowing which one to chase when he saw so many, went home again without having caught anyone.

Mr Owl watched it all from high, and he thought it was the funniest sight he had ever seen.

They had outwitted the wolf who never stole from them again.

A short time later,
the Easter Bunny was just
turning in for the night when
there was a "Tap-tap," at his
door.

He opened the door wide and
hopped outside.

And oh my, what a
wonderful sight he saw!

All the animals had gathered together for a surprise party. And his beautiful colorful painted Easter eggs were everywhere!

He felt very happy. Thanks to all of his friends, the Easter Bunny was able to leave eggs at every house he passed. And as he went hippety-hop along, he said to everyone

"Thank you for your help!"

On Easter morning, all the animals found Easter Eggs in their homes, in their nests, and dens and in the most unexpected places.

They all had a very Happy Easter.

The End

Printed in Great Britain
by Amazon